Turkey Trouble

by Wendi Silvano

illustrated by Lee Harper

two lions

Amazon Publishing, Attn: Amazon Children's Publishing, P.O. Box 400818, Las Vegas, NV 89140
www.amazon.com/amazonchildrenspublishing

Library of Congress Cataloging-in-Publication Data
Silvano, Wendi J.
Turkey trouble / by Wendi Silvano; illustrated by Lee Harper. — 1st ed. p. cm.
Summary: As Thanksgiving Day approaches, Turkey nervously makes a series
of costumes, disguising himself as other farm animals in hopes that he can avoid
being served as Thanksgiving dinner.
ISBN 978-0-7614-5529-5
[1. Turkeys—Fiction. 2. Costume—Fiction. 3. Domestic animals—Fiction.
4. Farm life—Fiction. 5. Thanksgiving Day—Fiction.] I. Harper, Lee, 1960- ill. II. Title.
PZ7.S585645Tur 2009
[E]—dc22
2008003186

The illustrations are rendered in watercolor on
140 pound Arches hot press watercolor paper.
Book design by Anahid Hamparian
Editor: Robin Benjamin

Printed in Mexico
First edition

To Dad . . . who inspires courage, endurance, and love
—W.S.

To Krista, Naomi, Nathan, Will, and Dan
—L.H.

Turkey was in trouble. *Bad* trouble. The kind of trouble where it's almost Thanksgiving . . . and you're the main course.

But Turkey had an idea. . . .

What if he didn't look like a turkey?
What if he looked like a horse?
Surely Farmer Jake wouldn't eat a horse for Thanksgiving.

His costume wasn't bad.
In fact, Turkey looked just like a horse . . . almost.

"Mooooo . . . ," said Cow. "Stop horsing around, Turkey."
"How'd you know it was me?" moaned Turkey.
"Too short," said Cow.
"Gobble, gobble," grumbled Turkey.

But looking at Cow gave Turkey a new idea. Surely Farmer Jake wouldn't eat a cow for Thanksgiving.

His costume wasn't bad.
In fact, Turkey looked just like a cow . . . almost.

"Oink . . . oink . . . oink," snorted Pig. "Holy cow! Is that you, Turkey?"
"How'd you know it was me?" groaned Turkey.
"Too skinny," said Pig.
"Gobble, gobble," grumbled Turkey.

But looking at Pig gave Turkey a new idea.
Surely Farmer Jake wouldn't eat a pig for
Thanksgiving.

His costume wasn't bad.
In fact, Turkey looked just like a pig . . . almost.

"Baaaa . . . baaaa . . . ," bleated Sheep.
"Quit being a ham, Turkey."

"How'd you know it was me?" wailed Turkey.
"Too clean," said Sheep.
"Gobble, gobble," grumbled Turkey.

But looking at Sheep gave Turkey a new idea.
Surely Farmer Jake wouldn't eat a sheep for Thanksgiving.

His costume wasn't bad.
In fact, Turkey looked just
like a sheep . . . almost.

"Cock-a-doodle-doo!" crowed Rooster. "Baaa-d idea, Turkey."

"How'd you know it was me?" howled Turkey.

"Too brown," squawked Rooster.

"Gobble, gobble," grumbled Turkey.

But looking at Rooster gave Turkey a new idea. In fact, it was his best idea yet. He already looked *a lot* like Rooster. This costume would be easy!

Surely Farmer Jake wouldn't eat a rooster for Thanksgiving . . .

. . . or would he?

Rooster might be his next choice, Turkey worried, *since roosters and turkeys look so much alike. Oh, gobble, gobble!*

Farmer Jake came into the barn.
"Turkey, turkey, turkey?
Come out, come out, wherever you are."

"Where's the turkey?" asked Farmer Jake's wife.
"I don't know," he said. "I looked everywhere!"
"Oh, dear. What will we do without a turkey for Thanksgiving?"
"Well . . . we could always eat the rooster, I guess."

Oh, no, not Rooster! thought Turkey.
He looked around desperately for one more idea.

Then, he found it. . . .

His costume wasn't bad. . . .
In fact, it was Turkey's best yet!
Ding-dong . . .
"Happy Thanksgiving!"

"Did you order a pizza?"
asked Farmer Jake's wife.
"Nope," he said. "But it's a good idea."

So they all sat down and gobbled up the pizza.

And it was Turkey's best Thanksgiving ever!